May the light on each candle bring you peace and happiness throughout the year. Happy Hanukkah!! Yours Truly,

Ms. Elise, Ms. Cristina, Mrs. Artura

Happy Reading! Please feel free to write a review on AMAZON-Grammar Hound's Mystery in Sentence City

Dear MZ,
Happy Hanukkah!
♡ Mrs. Artura
Ms. Elise
Ms. Cristina

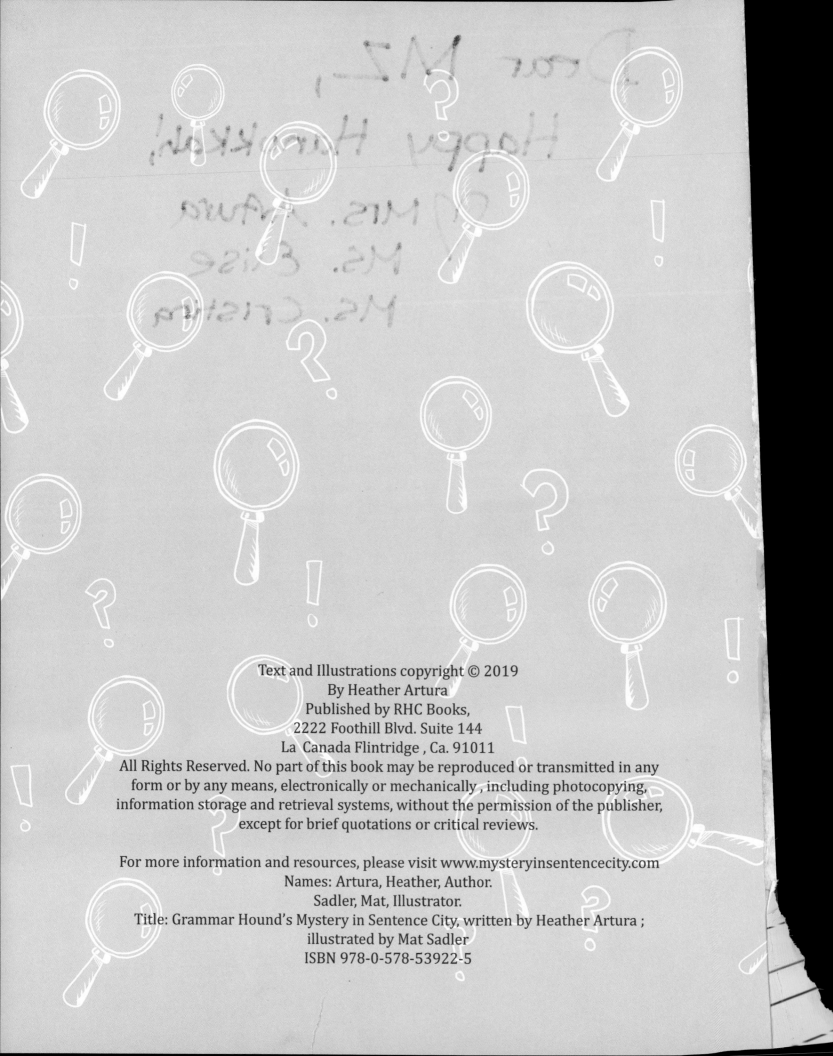

Text and Illustrations copyright © 2019
By Heather Artura
Published by RHC Books,
2222 Foothill Blvd. Suite 144
La Canada Flintridge , Ca. 91011

For more information and resources, please visit www.mysteryinsentencecity.com
Names: Artura, Heather, Author.
Sadler, Mat, Illustrator.
Title: Grammar Hound's Mystery in Sentence City, written by Heather Artura ; illustrated by Mat Sadler
ISBN 978-0-578-53922-5

Grammar Hound's
Mystery in Sentence City

By entering this book, you agree to follow the 3 Rules of Sentence City or you may be issued a Fix-It Ticket.

Fix-It Ticket

Did you...
1. Capitalize first letter in sentence? ☑
2. Add a finger space between each word? ☑
3. Put proper punctuation at the end of each sentence? ☑

By Heather Artura
Illustrated by Mat Sadler

Everyone in Ms. Oxford's class had an opinion about bugs.

"They're cool!" exclaimed Edward.

"They're weird," mumbled Madison.

"They're important," declared Zoe.

"Those are wonderful adjectives," said Ms. Oxford. "I would like you to write a sentence about bugs, and pin your page on the corkboard. Don't forget the 3 Rules of Sentence City."

Edward wrote,

bugs are really cool and creepy.

Madison wrote,

Mysister isalways scared thatabug will land onherhead.

Zoe wrote,

Some bugs do very important things. They co even make honey What would we do without bugs.

4

Ms. Oxford stood back and read the pages her students had pinned on the board.

"You have written some good sentences," she said. "But I'm afraid some things are missing."

"What things?" asked Edward.

"That is a mystery we're going to have to solve," Ms. Oxford said. "First, we need to figure out exactly what we are missing. Then, we will need some help finding those things."

"Were the things stolen?" Madison asked. "Maybe we should call the police!"

Ms. Oxford smiled. "That's a good idea, Madison. I know a police officer who might help us."

The door opened and a man came inside. He was tall and dressed in a blue uniform with shiny, gold buttons.

"It's Officer Wiseman!" exclaimed Madison.

"I remember when you taught us Good Citizenship in assembly," said Zoe.

Officer Wiseman smiled. "That's right," he said. "And how can I help you today?"

The children all began talking at once.

"Something's missing!"
"We were writing about bugs and created a mystery!"
"We need clues!"
"We have to hunt them down!"

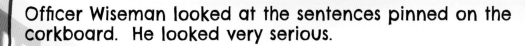

Officer Wiseman looked at the sentences pinned on the corkboard. He looked very serious.

"Oh, yes. Ah. I see. Yes, quite a complicated mystery here. Many things to track down. We need to see the capital."

"See the what?" asked Madison.

"Find the space," Officer Wiseman continued.

"Like outer space?" asked Edward, his eyes wide.

"And we'll need an Ask-Tell detector. Oh my. We'd better get started right away."

7

"That's a big place," said Zoe. "How will we find all the things we're missing? We don't even know what to look for yet."

Officer Wiseman smiled.

"Come outside," he said. "My partner is especially good at tracking things down."

Officer Wiseman's black and white van was parked next to the playground. Someone was sitting on the grass waiting patiently.

The dog looked up at the children, wagging his tail. His eyes were bright, his nose wet, and his brown ears so long they almost touched the ground.

"Close," Officer Wiseman said. "He's a Grammar Hound. His name is Henry, and he's very friendly. Now climb aboard, everyone. We don't want you to be late for lunch!"

It was a short trip to Sentence City, especially with Henry the Grammar Hound aboard.

But when the van stopped, it was time to get out.

The kids had arrived in Sentence City.

"Now Ms. Oxford," Officer Wiseman said. "Tell me when you first noticed something was missing."

"Well," she said, "something didn't seem right as soon as we read Edward's sentence."

"Good thing I brought all the papers along," Officer Wiseman said, pulling the sheets of paper from his shirt pocket.

By entering this land, you agree
to follow the rules of Sentence City
or you may be issued
with a Fix-it Ticket.

bugs are
really cool
and creepy.

"Hmmm," said Officer Wiseman. "There does seem to be something missing."

"How can we look for something, if we don't know what it is?" Edward asked.

"Let's ask my partner," Officer Wiseman said. He held the paper out to Henry, who sniffed it, standing very still and holding his tail straight up.

Suddenly, Henry began to bark and pull on his leash.

"He's got something!" Officer Wiseman exclaimed. "Everyone follow him!"

Henry trotted quickly down the sidewalk, and turned onto Rule Street.

When the kids turned the corner, they stopped.

"Wow!" Edward said. "Look at all the cool buildings!"

"That one looks like a giant O," Madison said excitedly.

"The one next to it looks like a big T," Zoe said. "Where are we?"

"These are the capital buildings of Sentence City!" Officer Wiseman declared. "The Grammar Hound must think we can find what's missing right here. Let's look again."

17

The Grammar Hound lifted his nose and sniffed. Then he lifted his tail and trotted over to a small tree. He looked up and began to bark.

"There's something in the tree," Edward said.

"Ah yes, I see it. Good job, Edward!" Officer Wiseman exclaimed.

"But what is it?" asked Madison.

It looked like a round basket with a hole in the middle.

"This," Officer Wiseman said, "is a B Hive. I think what you're looking for is inside."

Ms. Oxford carefully reached inside and pulled something out. She held it up for the children to see.

"It's the letter b!" Edward said, holding his paper. "But my sentence isn't missing one."

19

"This B Hive can only be found in the capital of Sentence City," Officer Wiseman said. "Does anyone know why?"

"Because it only has capitals!" Zoe said.

"That's exactly right," Ms. Oxford said. "Does anyone remember the first rule of building a sentence?"

"Start with a capital letter!" Edward said, excitedly.

20

"That's right," Officer Wiseman said. "The Grammar Hound found what your sentence was missing."

Edward carefully took the B from Ms. Oxford. He stuck it to his paper over the first letter.

Bugs are
really cool
and creepy.

"Mystery solved!" Officer Wiseman announced. "But we still have two more to track down."

He unfolded Madison's paper and held it out to the Grammar Hound. Henry sniffed and sniffed and even gave it a little lick with his pink tongue.

Then he turned and raced across the grass toward a lake.

"Are we going swimming?" Zoe asked.

But Henry stopped near the edge of the lake. He looked down at something. He jumped and barked, his tail wagging madly.

When the kids reached the lake, they all started talking at once.

"What is that? Is it a boat?" asked Edward.

"It's round like a flying saucer!" Madison said.

"Do you mean it's a UFO?" asked Zoe, taking a step back.

"You're on the right track," Officer Wiseman said. "This is Sentence City's very own spaceship."

"A spaceship? Can we go inside?" Edward asked.

Officer Wiseman smiled, and leaned over to push a button on the ship. A door opened and a little bridge popped out. Henry ran over the bridge and into the spaceship.

"One at a time," Officer Wiseman said. "Don't worry. It's quite safe."

Inside the ship, everything was shiny and smooth. It was empty except for a box in the middle of the floor.

"Ah, yes, I think I understand," Officer Wiseman said. "Madison, may we see your sentence?"

Madison unfolded her paper and gave it to him.

Mysister isalways
scared thatabug
will land onherhead.

Henry jumped up and put his paws on the box, his tail wagging wildly.

"Good boy, Henry," said Officer Wiseman. "Ms. Oxford? Would you like to give it a try?"

Ms. Oxford smiled and took Madison's paper. She smoothed it out, then slid it into the box. It dropped inside, just like a letter in a mailbox.

"What is that thing?" Madison asked.

"It's called a Space Maker," Officer Wiseman said. "All spaceships have them."

Suddenly, the Space Maker went silent and a piece of paper popped out.
"It's my sentence," said Madison. "But the paper got all stretched out."
My sister is always scar-ed that a bug will land on her head.

My sister is always scared that a bug will land on her head.

"Does anyone remember the second rule of building sentences?" Ms. Oxford asked.

"Always use a finger-space between each word!" Madison answered.

"Exactly!" Officer Wiseman said. "Your sentence was missing spaces, and the Grammar Hound knew how to find them." Everyone cheered with excitement!

"But we still have one more mystery to solve," said Ms. Oxford.

"Mine!" Zoe said.

Some bugs do very important things. They can even make honey. What would we do without bugs.

"I see all of Zoe's sentences begin with capital letters," Madison added.

"Zoe doesn't need any spaces," said Edward sadly.

"Yes, Edward, but now that you know where the spaceship is, you can come back anytime," Officer Wiseman said. "For now, let's see if the Grammar Hound can work his magic one more time."

Zoe held her paper out and Henry sniffed it.

First, Henry sniffed one side of the paper, then, the other. He held his tail absolutely still. Then he lifted his nose, his big ears swinging back. Henry's claws made clickety-clack sounds on the floor as he ran out the door.

The children laughed as they followed the Grammar Hound across the grass. Who knew fixing sentences could be so much fun?

Henry was heading for a small round
building painted a cheerful, bright red.
Over the large window was a sign:

Information

Officer Wiseman opened the door to the little building.

"Let's go inside and have a look!" he said.

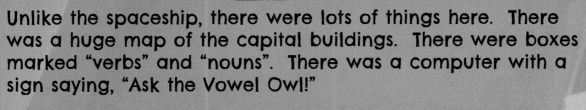

Unlike the spaceship, there were lots of things here. There was a huge map of the capital buildings. There were boxes marked "verbs" and "nouns". There was a computer with a sign saying, "Ask the Vowel Owl!"

"There are lots of cool things here," Edward said.

"But which one is for us?" Madison asked.

Henry trotted over to Zoe and sniffed her paper again. Then, he dove under a small table. He came back out with something in his mouth.

"I'll take that. Thank you, Henry," said Officer Wiseman.

"What is it?" Zoe asked.

Officer Wiseman held it up. It was the size of a small book, with several buttons and lights. In the middle was an arrow under a glass cover.

"This is an Ask-Tell Detector," he told the children.

"How does it work?" asked Edward.

"It tells us something important we need to know when we finish writing a sentence," said Ms. Oxford. "Who remembers the third rule of how to build a sentence?"

The children looked at one another.

Henry nudged the Ask-Tell Detector with his nose. Then he gave three short barks.

"Wuff! Wuff! Wuff!"

Madison laughed. "He sounds like he's asking, 'What? What? What?'"

37

"Oh, that's it!" Madison exclaimed. "The third rule - proper puncuation! Is it an asking sentence or a telling sentence?"

"That's right!" Ms. Oxford said, smiling.

"The Ask-Tell Detector is perfect for the job," Officer Wiseman said. "Zoe, hold your paper up."

Zoe held her paper in the air.

"Now Zoe has actually written three sentences," he explained. "So we will have to use the detector three times."

Some bugs do very important things. They can even make honey. What would we do without bugs.

SYNONYM ROLLS!

speak/talk | hot/cap | clever/smart | fast/quick

ANTONYM ANTS

small TINY

He pointed the Ask-Tell Detector at the first sentence. It made a buzzing sound, then the arrow spun to the left. The kids crowded around Officer Wiseman.

"It changed!" Edward exclaimed.

Zoe held the paper up.

What would we do without bugs?

"We did it! We found all the missing things!" Zoe declared.

"But we didn't use the Ask-Tell Detector on the middle sentence," Edward said.

Zoe read the sentence carefully.

They can even make honey.

"We don't need to," Zoe said. "It is a telling sentence. It has a period at the end. Nothing is missing."

"Can we do it anyway? I like the noises it makes," Edward said.

"Sure!" Officer Wiseman said.

Some bugs do very tint things. They can even make honey. What would we without bugs?

He pointed the Ask-Tell Detector at the middle sentence. The arrow began to spin around.

The Detector rang like a bell, then sang like a horn.

"What is it doing?" Edward asked. "It is so loud!"

"It sounds like you're winning a prize at the carnival," Zoe said.

"Hmmm," said Officer Wiseman. "Then we still have a mystery. Zoe has written a telling sentence. She put a period at the end of the sentence. But the Ask-Tell Detector is acting strangely."

The children looked carefully at the Detector. The arrow was pointing to TELL.

So what was it trying to tell them?

"Hey, a green button lit up," Madison said.

"Interesting," Officer Wiseman said. "Let's see what happens if I push that button."

He pointed the Ask-Tell Detector at Zoe's paper and pressed the green button. A little beam of green light flashed onto the paper.

"What did it do?" Edward asked.

"Do we have to leave Sentence City?" Madison asked.

"So soon?" Edward added.

"I think if we would like, Officer Wiseman can arrange for another visit to Sentence City, but only if we can remember the 3 rules of writing," Ms. Oxford said.

"With Henry too?" asked Edward.

Officer Wiseman smiled.

"Of course," he said. "I love to visit Sentence City and I never go without my Grammar Hound. You never know what he's going to find!"

THE END

COME
BACK
SOON

GRAMMAR
DETECTIVE

ANTONYM FARM
NEXT
LEFT

About the Author

Heather was raised in Danville, California and moved to Los Angeles in 1995 after graduating from college. She is a passionate educator with more than 20 years of classroom experience. She enjoys being creative, inspiring children with a love of knowledge and motivating them to explore their talents. In her spare time, Heather enjoys spending time at the beach with her husband Robert, her two children, Chase and Reese, and her dog Lucky.

She dedicates this book to her family, friends and her past and current students.